J **FRENCH**

or

s

Kick Back

£3.99

L 5/9

For Fairfield Grammar School, Bristol
1898-1998
Love from Viv

Barrington Stoke has enchanted and inspired
generations with his stories. He would go from village
to village, arriving at twilight and carrying a lantern
to light his way and signal his arrival. In the village
meeting place he set down his lantern and placed five
stones in a circle. Barrington Stoke stood at the front
of the circle in the light of his lantern. In the flickering
light the children sat entranced while he told the tale.
And then another. And then another, until they were
tired and ready for sleep. But Barrington Stoke's
imagination was never exhausted - he moved on to
the next day, the next village, the next story.

First published in Great Britain by Barrington Stoke Ltd
10 Belford Terrace, Edinburgh, EH4 3DQ
Copyright © 1998 Vivian French
Illustrations © Jake Abrams
The moral right of the author has been asserted in accordance
with the Copyright, Designs and Patents Act 1988
ISBN 1-902260-02-3
Printed by Polestar AUP Aberdeen Limited
Printed 1998 (three times) and 1999 (once)

Contents

Chapter One

Hi! I'm Josh Wilson - super star!

Who?

OK. I'm just Josh. And I'm not a super star. Not at all. Although you never know ... things are changing!

How?

I'll tell you. It started with Dad and the drum kit.

Your Dad plays drums?

No! Look, I'd better begin at the beginning.

Yeah. Good thinking.

I've never liked school much. I've never had kids fighting to be my friend. I've always thought it was because I've got big ears and big feet, but I don't know. I guess I've never been the chatty type. I'm not great at lessons either. Or games.

If I try to kick a ball I fall over - usually in the mud. I'm not interested in drama, and I don't want to play chess. All in all, school doesn't do much for me. I don't mind, but Dad does. Dad wants me to be Mr Popular - like he was when he was at school. That's why he bought me the drums.

Wow! Is your Dad rich?

Dad's a designer. He earns enough to go wild sometimes. I think he sometimes buys me stuff because he worries about me. Mum walked out

years ago, but he still thinks he has to look after me twice over.

So what happened with the drums?

Don't think I wasn't pleased. I was - I mean, doesn't everyone want a drum kit? This was a good one, too. Bass, snare, two tomtoms, high hat - the lot. And Dad was right. I suddenly found I had loads of friends. Everyone wanted to come home with me and try out being a drummer. Dad was really pleased.

He's got a huge studio for work, and he let me set up the drums at one end. Then he gave me an old kettle so we could make coffee or tea. He put out a huge tin of biscuits as well. The kids thought it was great. They took to dropping in after school, and at weekends.

Dad never noticed that it was the biscuits and the drums they came for, not me.

Sometimes they didn't talk to me at all, but sat around chatting to each other. I didn't mind. I got to know a lot more about school, and what was going on. And there was a gang of girls who came.

A gang of girls?

They always came together. Lily and Ruby were sisters. I never could remember which was which to begin with. Then I worked out that Lily was the LONG one, and Ruby was the ROUND one. Lily was older than Ruby, and bossed her about. Then there was Em. She was Lily's best friend. She had blond hair in a pony tail, and she was always tossing her head about. I reckon she thought she was really something. She bossed Ruby about too, and moaned at her. Moaning Em!

Who else was in the gang?

Alice. I quite liked Alice.

OK, OK. I thought Alice May was the best thing ever invented. She was amazing. Her skin sort of glowed, and she had these deep dark eyes that made my stomach flutter. Whenever she walked into the studio my knees went wobbly and my mouth hung open like a goldfish. I couldn't talk properly, and I knew my ears grew another two sizes every time I looked at her.

It was because of Alice that I began to play the drums seriously. I wanted to impress her. I thought she might like me if I could suddenly show her what a cool dude I was, even if I did have elephant ears. The trouble was the plan just did not work. Even when I got quite good I couldn't play if Alice was around.

I dropped my sticks and muddled up the beat and got everything wrong. I knew she was laughing at me. She and Moaning Em and Long Lily would get in a little huddle together and giggle. When she wasn't there I was miles

better. Ruby said I was good, but I think she was just being nice.

H'mmmm ... ?

No. I know what you're thinking, but Ruby was nice to everybody. She even washed up the dirty coffee cups before she went home. Nobody else ever did that. She talked to me, too. She told me all about Lily and Em.

And Alice?

Yeah - OK. And about Alice. But not as much as I wanted. Anyway, Ruby told me how Lily sang and played the guitar, and Em was a star on keyboards. She said that they used to belong to a band called White Lilies. I wanted to ask if Alice was in the band too, but I couldn't. Instead I asked what happened.

Ruby shrugged.

'Two of the other kids in the band moved away. Em and Lily are setting it up again, though.' She grinned. 'I'm going to play bass guitar.'

'I didn't know you could play,' I said.

'You never asked,' Ruby said. 'We'll be playing next Monday. You should come.'

'Maybe,' I said.

I didn't tell Ruby I'd never been to the youth club. Dad was always telling me how he'd had such FUN at the clubs he went to. It sort of put me off. I didn't think I'd have fun. Who'd want to talk to a geek with big ears and nothing to say? But I began wondering about it all the same ...

Bet you wondered if Alice would be there ...

Of course I did.

Chapter Two

I went to the youth club. I nearly didn't because I couldn't decide what to wear. Dad gave me a funny look when I changed my T-shirt for the third time, but he didn't say anything.

The club was packed. I knew most of the kids, and some of them said 'Hi!' and some of them didn't. They were mostly chatting, or playing snooker. I couldn't see Ruby or Lily. Or Alice. It all seemed a waste of time. I was thinking of going when I saw Em. She was carrying a big, black case - her keyboards!

Everything started happening then. A second later Lily came crashing in, and Ruby rushed in after her.

'Sorry!' Lily shouted at Em. 'The bus was late!'

And they swung into action, heaving chairs about and clearing a space.

'Wow! It's the Spice Girls!' a tall boy said, and a lot of people laughed.

Em and Lily and Ruby took no notice. They set up the speakers and the electric stuff really fast. I was impressed. They knew what they were doing. I wouldn't know one end of a wire from another, but they were plugged in and ready to go in under ten minutes.

'Lights!' Lily shouted, and Ruby dashed across the room.

The main lights dimmed, and a spot light switched on.

I don't know what I'd been expecting. Something girly, I think. Folky, dingly dangly

sort of music, anyway. But it wasn't. Lily wasn't brilliant on guitar - mostly basic chords - but she could sing. She had a really deep, gutsy voice, and it made shivers go up and down my spine. Em was good on keyboards, too. And Ruby was a surprise. She didn't try anything too clever, but she made a stunning sound.

Yes, I was impressed. I actually forgot about Alice for the whole of the first song, and I clapped like mad when they finished. They weren't genius level, but they did have something.

The next song wasn't good. Lily forgot her words, and Em was all over the place. And it got worse. After twenty minutes or so Lily and Em were arguing and the kids watching were moving away. Ruby stood up.

'It's no good,' she said. 'We need more rehearsals. We'll never get it together if we don't practise.'

'We DO practise,' Lily said. 'What do you

think we were doing all last night?'

'Only goes to show YOU weren't doing much,' Em said.

Ruby looked cross. 'I was doing as much as you. And it's your rhythm that's all up the creek.'

'RUBBISH!' Em shouted.

'Actually,' said a voice, 'she's right.'

Em looked as if she was about to burst. She leapt round to see who had spoken, and then froze. She went bright pink, and gave a little laugh.

'Oh. Hi, Ace. Hi.'

I couldn't see Ace at first, but then he lounged out of the darkness. He didn't walk. He was more like a tiger, or a panther. He was wearing a really cool, black leather jacket, and a sparkly stud in his ear. He looked at least sixteen or seventeen. Even I could see he was a hunky kind of guy. It was so obvious Em and Lily thought so too that I nearly laughed.

'You need more rhythm,' Ace said. 'Drums.' He tapped out a beat on the back of a chair. 'Hold it all together.'

'I'm sure you're right,' Lily said. Her voice had changed. It was all breathy.

'Yeah. Well.' Ace moved away. 'And more practice.' He jerked his head at Ruby. 'That kid's got sense. And she can play.' He stopped for a moment. 'If you got a drummer you'd be OK.' He nodded at Lily. 'Great voice, Lily.' And he lounged off.

There was a long pause. Lily and Em looked as if they'd had a personal visit from an angel. Ruby had a soppy grin on her face.

'Who was that?' I asked.

'Ace,' Lily said, and she gave me the 'Are you a COMPLETE moron?' stare.

'Oh,' I said. I waited to see if she was going to tell me any more, but she didn't. It was Ruby who took pity on me.

'He's a drummer. He's fab. He played on a tour with the Poppyheads when he was only fourteen.'

'Oh,' I said again. I wasn't sure that I'd ever heard of the Poppyheads. 'Ah.'

Ruby sighed. 'It would be great if he'd join us.'

'Why don't you ask him?' I said.

Ruby pulled me away from Lily and Em and began to whisper. 'Lily did ask him, but he said he didn't have his own drum kit. He said we'd have to buy him one. Like we could! Then she

asked him again, and he said he was too busy!' Ruby snorted. 'Lily was gutted! She thought he fancied her, and she was going to show off like mad when we play at Alice's party!'

It was my turn to look as if an angel had spoken. 'Alice is having a party?'

'Where have you been? Under a stone? She's having a HUGE party. And we're playing at it. Why do you think Lily and Em are so uptight? We'll be dead if we don't get ourselves sorted by then. The whole school will die laughing.'

'Oh.' I swallowed hard.

At that moment the band's problems were a zillion miles away. ALICE WAS HAVING A PARTY! How did I ask if I was invited? What if I wasn't? A sudden vision of Alice in party gear rushed into my head, and nearly blew it off.

'It's all right,' Ruby said, and she patted me as if she was my granny. 'You're invited. It's here, by the way.'

'What?'

Ruby shook her head sadly. 'Everyone knows you're besotted with her. Can't think why. She's a creep. But she'll expect you. She likes having you gazing at her like a lovesick puppy. Yuk.' And she giggled.

'Josh!'

I turned round. My head was spinning. Alice May knew I liked her! Was that good? Was it bad?

'JOSH!' It was Lily. 'Did you hear ANYTHING that I just said?'

'Er ... no,' I said.

Lily gave a heavy 'What An Idiot' sigh.

'I was asking you if you'd like to join us. White Lilies. The band. Be our drummer. You know what I mean? Play the drums? Boom boom boomitty boom?'

My jaw dropped so far I was surprised it didn't hit my feet. 'What?'

'Yes. He will. Won't you, Josh?' It was Ruby. She was answering for me while I got my head back together. I was in an advanced state of shock, but even so I noticed Ruby was nearly as surprised as me.

'Er ... yes. Yeah. Great,' I said. I gulped. 'Er ... great.'

Em gave me a sour look. 'If you're going to play with us you'll have to kill the goldfish look.'

'Er ... sorry,' I mumbled.

'Good,' said Lily. She gave me a brisk smile. 'And we'll rehearse at your place. Tomorrow evening. Seven, OK?'

'Er ... Yes. I mean great. Er ... fine,' I said.

Lily and Em didn't say another word. They packed up their stuff and went. Ruby winked at me, and followed them.

'See you tomorrow,' she called.

I nodded. Then I went home, and I went the wrong way twice. I was in a state of shock.

Chapter Three

Dad was waiting for me.

'Had a good time?' he asked.

'OK,' I said, and I tried to keep the soppy smile off my face. 'Oh - Dad - some girls are coming round tomorrow night to rehearse. Um ... I've been asked to join a band. We've got a gig, too.'

Dad was great. He didn't leap straight in and ask masses of questions - though I knew he wanted to. He just bashed me on the back, and sent me off to bed.

I knew he was pleased, all the same.

So was I. I stared at myself in the bathroom mirror. Me! Josh Wilson! Playing in a band. And not just any old band. White Lilies - the band that was going to play at Alice's party!!!

A thought hit me between the eyes, and I nearly fell over. Maybe after the party Alice would look at me the way Em and Lily had looked at Ace ...

Wow. There was nothing else to say. WOW!!!! Josh Wilson had started to have a life.

Chapter Four

Things went back to normal the next day at seven o'clock. Em arrived first ... and she brought Alice with her. I asked them if they wanted a coffee or something, and Em said yes. Alice just nodded. I spilt the water and couldn't find any milk. They sat and whispered to each other. When I dropped the sugar Em said,

'Oh, for goodness sake!' and stared at me.

Lily and Ruby were late. They'd missed the bus again. We didn't start rehearsing until eight, and it was a disaster. Em and Lily kept changing

things. Ruby hardly said a word. I couldn't keep the beat together. I kept seeing Alice out of the corner of my eye, and it really put me off. She wandered about, peering at Dad's drawings. When she wasn't doing that she was winking and nodding at Em as if they had a secret. It was hopeless.

By ten everyone had had enough. I offered them some more coffee, but Lily said no. Alice called Em over into a corner and they went off into a fit of giggles. They kept looking over at me, and every time they did they giggled even more. I tried to pretend I didn't notice.

'I'd like some coffee,' Ruby said.

'We haven't got time,' Lily snapped. 'We'll miss the bus.'

'Oh, well,' Ruby said. 'Hey - Josh - is it OK if I leave my guitar here?'

I was so surprised that she was expecting to come again I didn't answer.

'We'll leave our stuff too,' said Lily.

'Just don't go messing with my keyboard,' Em said, and she and Alice went off into another sniggering fit.

Lily put on her jacket. 'Come on,' she said. 'Bye, Josh. See you tomorrow. Better make it six thirty.'

'Oh,' I said. 'Yeah.'

Em and Alice went out without saying anything. Ruby went out last. She made a horrible face at Em and Alice's backs and gave me a thumbs up sign as she went. I collapsed on a heap of old cushions. At that moment I wouldn't have minded if I'd fallen straight through them into the middle of Australia.

Chapter Five

It got a little better the next day. And the next. Alice didn't come again, and the sound began to work. Lily had the most amazing voice ... and Ruby did too. Ruby sang backing vocals. She wouldn't ever take the lead. Actually, Lily never gave her the chance.

We had been rehearsing for nearly two weeks when I noticed something odd. Lily and Em snapped and snarled at each other, and moaned and grouched at Ruby. Ruby didn't say

a lot, but she finally got fed up. Boy, did she throw a wobbly! And she threw it at everyone. Lily, Em, me. We were all USELESS!

It was then that I noticed. Em and Lily never grouched or moaned at *me.* They never told *me* to do something a different way. It was almost as if I, Josh, didn't exist ... I was just a beat. Just drums. It was odd. Really odd. In the end I asked Ruby about it. She gave me a funny look, and then she shrugged.

'They're cows, those two,' she said.

I was shocked. Of course I'd heard girls called cows - and much worse - before. It was the way Ruby said it. She sounded as if she really, truly meant it. I didn't ask any more, though. I thought maybe Lily and Em had been picking on Ruby at home or something. And I wasn't exactly complaining. It left me in peace and I was enjoying playing in a band so much I didn't want to change anything.

A couple of days later something else odd happened. Lily came in late, and Ace was with her. I went across to say hello, but Em stopped me.

'We ought to get started NOW. We don't have time to chat,' she said.

'Yes,' Lily said. 'Are you ready, Josh?'

Ace only stayed for a couple of numbers. He looked as if he was enjoying himself, so I was surprised when Lily stopped us.

'Ace has got to go now,' she said, and almost bundled him out of the door. Em went after her, and I raised my eyebrows at Ruby. Ruby wasn't looking at me. She was scowling at her guitar as if she hated it.

'Rube?' I said. 'What's the matter?'

'Cows,' she said. 'COWS!'

And then Em and Lily came back, and we went on rehearsing.

By the week of Alice's party we were good. I know that sounds as if I'm boasting, but it's true. I began to have massive fantasies about Alice staring at me in amazement.

'I never knew you were so talented!' she would say ... at least, she did in my head. To be honest, there was a whole lot more that went on in my head about Alice. You know the sort of thing.

The big row happened the day before the party. I woke up feeling sick with excitement - and nerves. We had a final rehearsal that afternoon. School had finished two days before; just as well, because I was brain dead.

We started rehearsing, and it sounded pretty good to me. I was well into it when Lily suddenly threw her guitar on the floor.

'That's it!' she yelled. 'I've had it!' And she turned on me.

'Can't you EVER hear a rhythm? I can't stand it any longer! You're throwing us all out of sync!'

Em crashed a horrible chord.

'Well,' said Lily. 'He's murdering the pace. Thump, thump, thump. It's AWFUL. ANYBODY could play better than him. He'll ruin it tomorrow -'

Lily swung round to Ruby. 'I always told you this was a naff idea. Just because YOU fancy a big-eared twerp WE get lumbered with a crap drummer -'

'Hey!' Ruby's face was scarlet. 'Leave me out of this!'

'NO!' Lily stamped her foot. 'I'll do better than that! We'll leave HIM out and find someone else! Josh Wilson - you're FIRED!!!!'

And she snatched up her guitar, hauled the lead out of its socket and stormed out.

I stared. I couldn't believe what had happened was for real. I sat there goggling as Em packed up her stuff. She flung me a freezing stare and flounced out. I couldn't even say anything to Ruby. If ever anyone was totally and utterly gobsmacked it was me, at twenty past two on a Friday afternoon.

Ruby was packing her guitar into its case with extraordinary care.

'Josh,' she said, and her voice was trembling. 'I'm really, really sorry. I promise you it wasn't my idea. It really, really wasn't anything to do with me.'

And then she went too.

When they'd gone I didn't know what to do. The studio felt worse than empty. It was hollow. In the end I washed up all the cups, very carefully. Then I packed all the drum kit away into its carrying cases. I did that very carefully too. Then I went to watch TV, and I couldn't tell you what I watched if you paid me a million pounds.

Lily phoned that evening. She spoke to Dad. I hadn't told him what had happened, so he came breezing up to my room.

'That was Lily. She said someone would be round to collect the drum kit early tomorrow morning. I asked if she wanted to speak to you, but she said not to bother you. Oh, and she said Ruby will see you at the party. And something about Alice is expecting you. Careful, lad!!'

Dad zapped back downstairs.

I sat and digested what he'd said. They were collecting my drums. MY drums. It was such incredible, barefaced cheek I had to get up and walk round to work it out. They were going to use my drums - without me. So who was going to play them? Who? WHO? Well, they couldn't. I wouldn't let them have them. I wasn't going to the party, and my drums weren't going either. Never, Never. NEVER.

That's what I said, but even as I stamped about I knew I was fooling myself. They could easily find some idiot or other who could bang out a rhythm. They didn't need me. They needed the drums.

And how could I ruin Alice May's party?

Chapter Six

I went to the party. I don't know why. I was
so torn in half I felt like two people walking into
the youth club. Half of me was curled up like a
tiny, boiled shrimp wanting to die. The other
half was - I don't know. Angry? Maybe. There
was something in my chest that felt as if it
might explode at any moment.

I'd managed to be out when they came round
for the drums. I don't know who came - it wasn't
a girl. Some bloke, Dad said.

That was terrible, too. I still hadn't told Dad
what had happened. He'd been so pleased with
the way things had worked out. He'd been

whistling for weeks. At last his son was one of the gang. Like he'd been. Popular. Chased by girls. I wish.

So - I went to the party. The room looked fantastic. Disco lights were flashing red and green and yellow in time to the music belting out of a huge sound system. There was a massive dry ice machine pumping out thick swirls of white fog, and there were kids everywhere. They were dancing and jumping about and shrieking and yelling.

As I pushed my way through them I saw the stage. It made me catch my breath. Em, Lily and Ruby were frozen against a sea of silver streamers. They were dressed in something that glittered and gleamed. Behind them were the drums, and behind the drums was ... Ace.

I knew then. It all made sense. Of course it did. Anyone else would have sussed it right from the beginning. Ace could play the drums. Ace didn't have any drums. Who did? Oh, of course.

Josh. And oh yes! That lovely studio! REHEARSAL
SPACE! And Josh is mad about Alice ... Easy!
Where's your basic maths? String Josh along -
get the rehearsing done - then BINGO! Drop him.
I did get angry then. Boiling ... but it was me I
was angry with.

What a sucker! What a wimp! FOOL! IDIOT!
It all came screaming through my head. And at
that moment the music stopped. So did the disco
lights. One single spot beamed down on Lily ...
and she was beautiful. I'd never noticed before.
But beautiful like a snake.

Or a bird of prey. Then she smiled, a killer of
a smile.

'Hi! We're here to tell you that White Lilies
are back - but we're different! We've changed!
Listen - and we'll show you!'

There was an expectant rumble and murmur
from the audience.

'Ready?' shouted Lily. 'One ... two ...' and the music crashed out.

And it was good. It was SO good. And Ace was ... I haven't got the words for it. He made the bass snarl and growl while the tomtoms rocked out the beat, and the snare sang. I shut my eyes to listen, and wait for Lily to come soaring in over the top. But she didn't.

The crowd rustled and muttered. I opened my eyes. Lily was standing at the mike like a

ferret looking down the barrel of a gun. Em was stabbing at the keyboard while she mouthed across at Lily. Ruby was staring. Only Ace was carrying on his thundering, crashing beat.

Lily had forgotten the words. I could tell. She had forgotten the words, and she was about to mess up the music. Maybe not the greatest music in the world - but something special. Special for me. Music that pounded in my head and in my heart and sent wild tingles up and down my spine.

The strange choking in my chest exploded. I leapt onto the stage and grabbed the mike. Lily's fingers were icy cold and clammy. She gave a strange little moan, and then she was off - legging it down the hall.

'Hey!'

I was shouting. I'd forgotten I was holding a powerful microphone. There was stunned silence, and below me was a sea of gaping mouths and staring eyes.

'Hey!' I said again. 'Now listen! All of you! That was White Lilies - as they used to be! But Lily told you changes had been made - and now you're going to hear them! I'd like to introduce you to - RUBY LILIES!'

Ace gave a crashing roll on the drums as I grabbed Ruby's wrist and hauled her to the mikes.

'Sing!' I hissed. 'Go for it!'

And I stared at Em. She had to make a split second decision. Did she play - or did she chuck the band and go with Lily?

Em played. Ace played. Ruby picked up her guitar and sang.

It wasn't anything like it might have been ... how could it? Voice, bass, keyboards and drums - not the ideal combo. But it had a strange haunting quality that caught the crowd. They were swaying, and smiling. And then it happened. From the back of the hall came an echo, and then a stronger harmonic twist of the tune. It was Lily. She came slowly back, weaving her way in and out of the crowd ... singing.

She reached the stage, and picked up her guitar ... and there it was. The total sound. Everyone in the hall froze. They were listening to the music. And the music was good. It was so good I couldn't breathe.

And I knew that was what mattered. I didn't care what games Lily and Em had been playing with me. In a way I understood - now. If you want something to be good - really good - you go for it. But Lily had nearly lost it, and I - big-eared Josh Wilson - had pulled it back into being! My head buzzed. It was me that had made this amazing noise happen ... me, who'd never done anything, ever.

After they'd finished playing they were cheered and clapped for ages. They sang 'Happy Birthday to you' to Alice, and she came onto the stage to smile at us all. She was right in front of me, and she smiled straight at me. And do you know what? It didn't mean a thing. I had discovered something extraordinary. I had discovered that I - Josh Wilson - had a passion in life and it wasn't Alice May. I found myself climbing onto the stage and heading for Ace. He clicked the drum sticks at me.

'Hi there. Feeling better?'

'What?'

Ace raised an eyebrow. 'Lily said you couldn't play. Flu. You look OK now.'

'Oh, I am,' I said. 'Quite OK. Better than OK. Great.'

'Fine.' Ace gave the snare a tickle or two. 'Nice fit out. Can I drop by your place sometime and have another go?'

I gulped. 'Yeah. Of course.'

'Cool,' Ace said. 'I liked your style. Show you some tips, if you like.'

'Great,' I said. 'Great.'

Ruby came over. 'Alice wants us to play again,' she said.

'Groovy,' said Ace, and he got up. 'Here you go, Josh. Your hot seat. Give it some power.'

And I did.

Other titles published by Barrington Stoke:-

Billy the Squid by Colin Dowland   1-902260-04-X

The Gingerbread House by *Adèle Geras*   1-902260-03-1

Virtual Friend by Mary Hoffman   1-902260-00-7

Wartman by Michael Morpurgo   1-902260-05-8

Screw Loose by Alison Prince   1-902260-01-5

For further information please contact Barrington Stoke at:-
10 Belford Terrace, Edinburgh EH4 3DQ